THIS

SWEET PICKLES

BOOK BELONGS TO

In the Town of Sweet Pickles, the animals get into and out of pickles because of their all too human personality traits.

Each of the books in the *Sweet Pickles* series is about a different pickle.

This book is about things that may not always be what they seem.

This story is for Sharon.

Library of Congress Cataloging in Publication Data

Perle, Ruth Lerner.
   The grand prize.
   (Sweet Pickles)
   SUMMARY: All astir about the coming school fund
raising and raffle, the animals of Sweet Pickles can't
read the signs posted by Zany Zebra who stands on his
head much of the time.
   [1. Zebras — Fiction.   2. Animals — Fiction]
I. Hefter, Richard, ill.   II. Title.
PZ7.P4324Gr   [E]   81-9767
ISBN 0-937524-10-7   AACR2

THE GRAND PRIZE

Written by Ruth Lerner Perle
Illustrated by Richard Hefter

Euphrosyne Incorporated

One afternoon, in the Town of Sweet Pickles, Healthy Hippo was jogging up Main Street. As he passed the town hall, he noticed a giant sign on the bulletin board.

Hippo slowed down to read the sign.

It said SNIM XIS.

He stopped jogging and looked at the sign again. It still said *SNIM XIS*.

Hippo sat down on the town hall steps and took three deep breaths. He put his stethoscope against his chest and listened to his heart. He felt his pulse. Then, he turned around and looked at the sign again. It definitely said SNIM XIS.

"I've been running too much," thought Hippo. "Or, maybe I haven't been running enough. Anyway, I'd better stop at the hospital to have my eyes checked. I probably need more vitamins."

Hippo walked slowly across Central Park. Another sign was tacked to a tree. Hippo looked at it with one eye. It said SNIM XIS. He looked at it with the other eye. It said SNIM XIS.

All over the park, on every bench, there were signs with SNIM XIS written on them in great big letters.

When Hippo arrived at the emergency entrance of the hospital, there was a big crowd waiting. Everyone was yelling and screaming and moaning. Worried Walrus was wiping his forehead. "Oh, dear, Hippo," he cried. "I am *so* worried. This is a *real* problem. Everywhere I go, I see SNIM XIS. Something terrible has happened to my eyes."

"Me too," sighed Imitating Iguana. "Something terrible has happened to my eyes, too."

"It's weird," wailed Doubtful Dog. "I thought I knew how to read, but now I doubt it. I can't make out any of the signs."

"You mean," whispered Bashful Bear, "you're having trouble, too? I thought I was the only one and I was afraid to mention it."

Then, Accusing Alligator came storming in. "Just as I suspected!" she screamed. "It's an epidemic! No question about it!"

"The question is," said Questioning Quail, "what's going on and what can we do about it?"

"I can answer those questions," laughed Zany Zebra, as he rode by on his skateboard.

"The annual School Fund Drive is what's going on. And what you can do about it, is buy some raffle tickets to support it.

"I have fifty raffles, numbers 1 through 50. If you buy a raffle, you will help our school. And, there's a grand prize for the one who gets the raffle with the winning number on it.

"Besides," smiled Zebra, "I personally guarantee that your eyes will feel better when it's time to award the prize."

Everyone bought raffles. Walrus bought ten of them. So did Iguana. "I sure hope this helps my eyes," sighed Walrus. "Me too," sighed Iguana.

When all the raffles were sold, Zebra said, "OK, everybody! Go home and come to Town Hall tomorrow morning. You will find out which number wins. You will see that there is nothing wrong with your eyes and don't forget...SNIM XIS!"

The next morning, everybody gathered on the Town Hall steps. Zebra was there, waiting for them. He smiled and said, "I'm happy to announce that we collected a lot of money for the School Fund."

Zebra did a hand-stand in front of the big sign. "And now," he called, "will the owner of the winning number please come up to claim the grand prize." Everyone looked around. Nobody knew what the winning number was. They started to grumble and complain.

Alligator marched up the steps and pointed at Zebra. "Listen, wise-guy!" she screamed. "We've had enough of your tricks! First, you put up signs we can't read, then you take our money, and now we don't know who the winner is!"

"You can tell who the winner is, if you'll just look at the sign," chuckled Zebra. "It's perfectly clear to me!"

"It looks like you're not giving away the grand prize!" sneered Alligator. "That's what's clear to me!"

Zebra stood on his head and waved his arms. "It's a matter of *how* you look at it," he grinned, "…it's all in your point of view."

Then, Zebra reached up and grabbed the SNIM XIS sign. He jumped right side up with it and held it up for everyone to see. The sign said SIX WINS. The crowd roared and cheered.

"And now," declared Zebra, "will the winner please step forward. Who has raffle number six?"

Walrus looked at his raffles. "I don't have number six," he said, "but my eyes feel a lot better."

"Me too," said Iguana.

Alligator threw her raffles away. "All right!" she shouted. "Who has number six?"

Nobody answered.

The crowd started to get angry again.

Then, a loud snore was heard. Everyone turned around to look.

There was Goof-Off Goose, snoozing in the sun.
A crumpled raffle was hanging out of her pocket.
It was raffle number six.

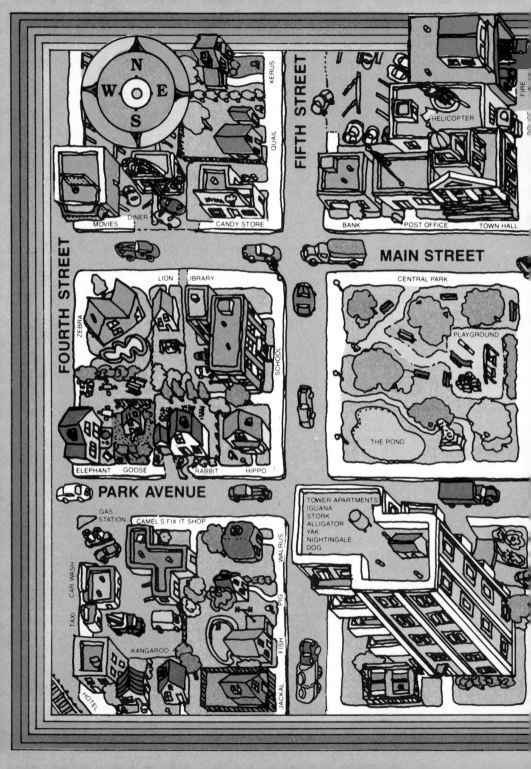